DATE DUE

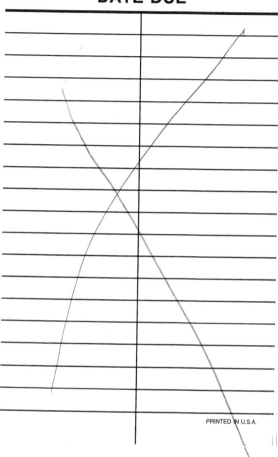

PRINTED IN U.S.A.

P

Owl's tree

Scruffy's field

Abbey ruins

Villag

Bertie's field

Poppy's field

Castle ruins

Standing Stones

Norah's field

Church

School

Dolly's field

Smiff's field

Zizi's field

Crow's Woods

For Douglas and Sophie

First Published in 1991
Text copyright © Tom Allen, 1991
Illustrations copyright © Patsy Allen, 1991

Photoset by Deltatype, Ellesmere Port
Printed in Italy
for J.M. Dent & Sons Ltd
91 Clapham High Street
London SW4 7TA

British Library Cataloguing in
Publication Data
Allen, Tom
  Scruffy.
  I. Title II. Allen, Patsy III.
Series
  823.914 [J]

The illustrations for this book were prepared using
water-colours.

THE RAINBOW SCARECROWS
Scruffy

Tom & Patsy Allen

DENT CHILDREN'S BOOKS
London

A few days after the great storm in Acorn Woods the little scarecrow Scruffy still lay under the hedge at the end of the barley field. It was raining again and the poor little scarecrow was dripping wet. Then at last the sun started to peep through. Suddenly an enormous rainbow appeared in the sky, shining brightly against the grey clouds. The rainbow's end touched the little scarecrow.

At that moment Scruffy felt the raindrops. He looked up at the sun and felt its warmth on his face. He stretched and smiled . . . Scruffy had come to life.

A robin fell out of Scruffy's hat as the scarecrow shook his shoulders and stiffly turned his straw head.

"Must be an earthquake!" the robin piped out.

Scruffy looked at the bird in amazement and stepped back, slipping right into a puddle.

"That wasn't very clever, was it?" laughed the robin in a friendly way.

"I'm sorry but I don't think I am very clever," said Scruffy, playing with the mud between his fingers.

T hen Scruffy began to giggle. He felt a
tickling in his tummy. One by one, four
little field mice popped their heads out of
his waistcoat, squeaking in alarm. They had
been living in a very comfortable nest in
Scruffy's pockets and wanted to know why their
home had started to roll about and talk!

"I can see you're going to get into all sorts of trouble unless you're looked after properly. The first thing we need to do is to take you to see Owl," said Robin.

"Who is Owl?" asked Scruffy as they all set off.

"Owl is a bird like me, only he's bigger and wiser," explained Robin. "He keeps an eye on all of us and we go to him if we need help."

They reached a large oak-tree in the middle of the wood and saw Owl perched on his favourite branch. Owl blinked at Scruffy with his huge round eyes and then he ruffled his tawny feathers.

"Oh, so you're here at last. We've been expecting you since we saw the special rainbow over the barley field. Come and meet the others."

"What others?" asked Scruffy in surprise. "The other Rainbow Scarecrows, of course," replied Owl. "Come inside."

"Let me introduce everyone. This is Smiff, Norah, Poppy, Bertie and Dolly . . . and Zizz is over there in the corner."

Owl explained to Scruffy how he and the Rainbow Scarecrows helped to look after Acorn Woods and all the woodland animals who lived there.

After tea it was time for them all to go back to their fields – they had a lot to do. Scruffy was the last to go. Owl went over to the corner and picked up an umbrella.

"This is yours now, Scruffy. Look after it carefully."
It was a fantastic umbrella made up of all the colours of the rainbow.

"Watch out for the crows!" called Owl, as Scruffy left for home. It was beginning to get dark and Scruffy felt a little uneasy.

"Don't worry Scruffy," chirped Robin. "It gets dark like this at the end of every day."

When Scruffy got back to his field, he dozed off quickly. But in the middle of the night he was woken up. A fox was sniffing around his legs. Scruffy stared down at him, but the fox just grinned. His sharp teeth and cunning eyes glinted in the moonlight. Then he turned and went on his way. Scruffy was sure he would get used to all the woodland creatures soon. He wasn't scared any more and he soon fell asleep again.

But at dawn he was woken by Robin and the mice, "Quick! Wake up! The crows are coming!"

The little scarecrow was startled and looked up as the huge black birds wheeled around him and then landed at his feet to feed. So these were the crows that Owl had warned him about. This time he was really frightened! His tummy began to flutter and his knees felt like jelly.

"Shoo! Go away!" he said, softly at first, then louder, and he waved his arms, "Boo! Be off with you!"

The crows just stared at him and laughed. They weren't scared of a little scarecrow.

Then Scruffy had an idea. It was his very first one. He reached for his umbrella and opened it . . .

Immediately the umbrella filled with air and took off, with Scruffy holding on tightly. He soared through the air, scattering the crows in all directions. They'd never seen anything like it, and they flew off as fast as they could, flapping their wings noisily and cawing loudly. Scruffy soon began to enjoy himself floating through the air on his magic umbrella.

He didn't really want to come down but the crows had gone, and so he drifted slowly back to earth. A group of animals gathered round him and started to clap and cheer as he landed.

"Well done! You're so brave!" they shouted.

"Oh it was nothing!" Scruffy answered, as he closed his rainbow-coloured umbrella. Secretly he felt very pleased with himself.

Just then Scruffy saw Owl flying towards him. Behind him followed six brightly-coloured umbrellas. Hanging from each umbrella was a scarecrow! As they landed next to Scruffy he recognized them – Dolly, Smiff, Bertie, Norah, Poppy and Zizz.

They all patted him on the back and shouted, "Well done, Scruffy! You're a real Rainbow Scarecrow now!"

Owl's tree

Scruffy's field

Abbey ruins

Villag

Bertie's field

Poppy's field

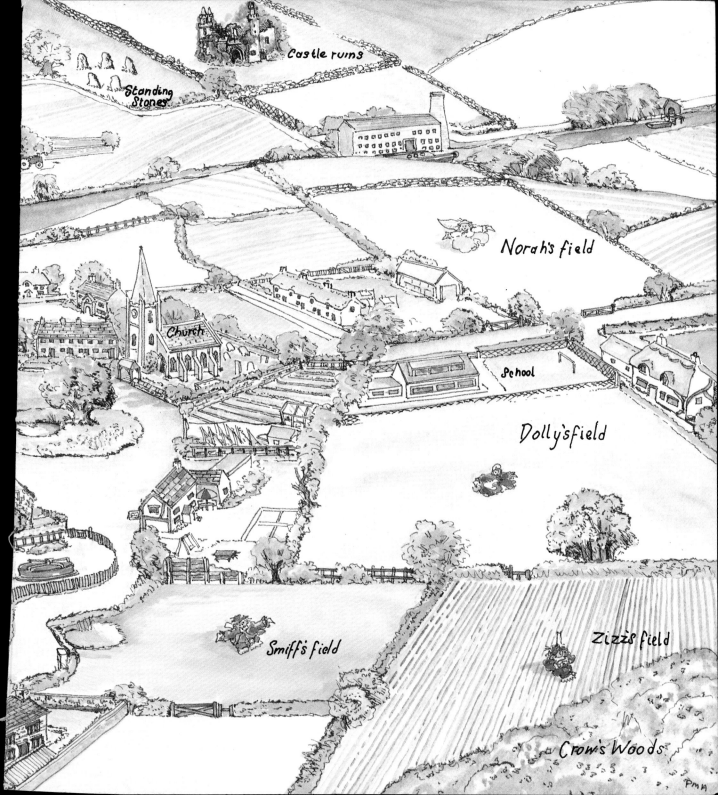

Castle ruins

Standing Stones

Norah's field

Church

School

Dolly's field

Smiff's field

Zizz's field

Crow's Woods